Thoughts from a naked, unshackled mind

Anno Nomius

Printed in the United States of America
First Printing: 2015

ISBN 978-0-9907412-9-9

NCIPB Inc,
PO Box 167
Stevenson, CT 06491-0167

stories.ncipb.com

Preface

If you picked this book (& I am glad you did), I can assure you that it will not be what you are expecting.

If you picked this book thinking that, finally there is, a book that tells you how to motivate yourself for each day of the week sorry this is not it.

However, if you picked this book with an open mind, & are looking for some fun & perspective in life, you will not be disappointed.

The way to read this book is slowly, first thing in the morning. Read a few pages at a time & spend the day musing about what you read. You could pick a topic or start anywhere you like - order does not matter, but remember to always have a beer in the other hand when reading. That is the most important piece of advice as you thumb through the pages!

This book is dedicated to the hard working citizens of the free world.

Happy Reading!

*Thank you **RBD** for the checks & balances even on the unshackled.*

Aloha

5 decades since JFK's inaugural address- it is time now to ask, what your country can do for you & not what you can do for your country. You, my friend have done enough!

Smoker to Smoker - Thank you Mr. President for normalizing relations with Cuba. Finally, we can get some good quality cigars.

At the pharmacy drive-through, keep a poker face, say that you are here for a pickup & your last name is Schwarzenegger, & have some fun at the frenzy that ensues.

A black cat crossing the road is considered bad luck in some cultures. What about the cat's culture?

Sumo wrestling - Let the fat fighting begin. You see a lot of skin in this game, *butt* you hope the mawashi (lion-cloth) does not come off; you are just are not prepared to see that much skin.

Have you ever been cut in line? What did you do? Swore under your breath or took out your imaginary gun. How about when someone took the parking spot, you were aiming for in a crowded lot.

Have you ever had an urge to pee or take a dump but could not, because of the circumstances? Interestingly, the simplest of activities give you so much relief, when accomplished.

You stand no chance if you are running alone, when chased by a mountain lion or grizzly bear. When chased, make sure you are in a group, & that you are not the slowest in the group.

Once heard a Yale alumni speaking to a group of underprivileged kids about his toughest life experience - it was about how he sweated profusely on his way to a job interview on Wall Street. Wow, some perspective!

You wonder who posts on Face-book & about what? Attention seeking queen bees posting pictures in sexy attires, updating the world about their fabulous life. Occasionally, you see an informative article, joke, a plagiarized adage, or proverb.

Some airheads & shallow individuals post such profound Face-book updates. You wonder whether it is an instance of plagiarism or if you labeled them right. Perhaps they were profound all along & you missed it. Even to steal, you have to understand the value of the stolen goods.

Queen Anne of England, managed to coax other people to give her things that took her fancy. Her dollhouse with dolls from around the world, which was a "gift," is testament.

A prostitute, vs. an escort - same age-old profession, but treated & paid differently.

Tornadoes & hurricanes are crazy & people, who stay put when these strike, are crazier.

Getting a tan, dealing with 90-degree temperatures on your skin - Looking good has never been more important, after the basic needs are met.

Interesting greetings around the world: the fist bump, hug, handshake, namaste with the folded hands, bowing of the head, cheek rub, single kiss, double kiss, air kiss ... & the list goes on.

Ask poor Peter what he will do with the $50 he just got. The answer will surprise you. Clothes's, looking good is the answer, not saving for a rainy day. When you are living hand to mouth, you only think of having a good time now. Who has seen tomorrow?

So much to do, so little time. Need to hurry. At the daily or hourly level, it seemed all was under control.

Highways, freeways, roadways, dirt road, expressway, parkway...all started in Rome or perhaps Greece.

Was the world as bad in the past, as it is today? Poverty, strife, genocide, wars... Wonder if anything will ever change or help drive change.

Scribes to take notes. When great men or men who think they are great, talk, somebody needs to take notes.

It's amazing how we believe, what we want to believe, & don't see the real facts staring at us. Tunnel vision at its best.

New Haven - New York of Connecticut. Gourmet food, celebrity chefs, lounges, good music, & theaters, alongside the occasional gunshots, mugging, & carjacking.

People with a sense of entitlement, continue to amaze. The pretty girl - who has a crowd of swooning men following her, the handsome man who has a bevy of women worshippers & when they don't get their way, they throw tantrums, each in their own special way.

Someone once said – "war is waged for profits."

So much strife & poverty in Africa. Too many tribes, with too much in fighting, for limited resources.

More often than not, the people who really make a difference in any endeavor go un-acknowledged. Look at the people who built the house you are living in. Know any of their names?

Class reunions are events to compare notes. Who's got the better job, more beautiful wife, richer husband, smarter kids, larger house…whose life is "better" than the other's is.

Competition never ceases. Survival of the fittest, & of course, with that, comes bragging rights.

Some people are so full of themselves, that they cannot fathom, that others do not give a hoot about them or what they have accomplished. *N'est-ce pas.*

The great American Indians. Now all they have is their casinos at the reservations, tobacco, & handicrafts. Few are well educated. Someone I knew dumped his American Indian girlfriend because she was not as educated as he was. Jerk.

Do you ever walk around with a surreal feeling- is this really me? Walking, waving, talking...

Wonder how many people ever think about, let alone follow, the teachings of Gandhi or Nelson Mandela. What is the point? They are both dead, as are their values of non-violence.

How did it feel to be verbally abused for the first time, or for that matter, anytime? Perhaps you were, making a left turn in front of a 'no left turn' sign, with a line of cars behind you, & someone hurled abuses at you or showed you the finger. You were probably thinking – "hope the same happens to you, jerk!" Will the lord hear your fervent prayers?

Is there anything you can buy at a dollar store that is safe to consume? Soap, Paper plates maybe.

Have you been on a $10 bus to Boston from NY? Then there is the $1 Big Bus from NY with a huge queue. Businesses' competing is good.

What is the most crowded place you have walked out of? Theatre? Classroom? A burning high-rise building? Perhaps you jumped in the last case. Crowds can be claustrophobic.

Crazy street names – is there a bank on "Bank Street"? Is there a river near "Riverside view"? What about city names? Is there at least a water-fall somewhere around Beacon falls?

Long, complicated names. Anagnostopoulos, Schwarzenegger, & the list go on. Then there are names which have a "!" - Remember N!xau, from the movie "The Gods must be crazy"? Consider naming your kid with an exclamation!

People dying in a "friendly" fire. How about "40 people died in a case of unintended firing". The term "blue on blue" is ok too.

When you meet a person who is clueless about the world, you think of a toad in his personal well. "You are from Africa do you know Tarzan? You went to school. Really? On an elephant?" A con-versation that can occur in College Station, TX or the deep redneck south, places where NY is still considered another country.

Wonder how that squirrel jumps up & down the tree branches so smoothly, but is inevitably crushed on the straight open road.

Raccoons can climb up the shingles to get to the roof, & it sounds like a human is scratching the walls. When this occurs at 2 am, you miss a heart-beat, think it's a thief, & call 911.

Would anyone want to live in Iceland in winter?

People find reasons to do the things they want to do, & justify it too. Everyone does it - normal people, murderers, adulterers, even the saints.

Have you counted the number of times the words "like" & "whatever" are used when teenage girls talk? Teenage boys, they just don't talk as much. They just do "stuff," harmful stuff with guns.

When kids have to battle cancer instead of homework, your heart goes out. I once knew a 17-year-old who died of cancer. The night he died, I wept.

Apollo 18 & the denials, Area 51 & the UFOs - keep us wondering about alien life and a lying government.

Facebook, Twitter, LinkedIn, Instagram, Pintrest, & our quest for connections goes on.

Typhoons, earthquakes, volcanoes, nature's wrath, & quest for destruction of everything in its path goes on.

We have yet to conquer nature. It continues to overwhelm - tsunamis, earthquakes, forest fires, volcanoes.

Devastation means different things to different folks - loss of a job, loss of a loved one in a giant landslide, losing your home & everything in it in a tsunami or earthquake, & for some, it could mean chipping a fingernail.

Farmer's markets - A pleasant escape from the cookie cutter culture of the supermarkets. Support fresh local produce & local farmers. Eat fresh & be healthy.

The mind keeps rambling thoughts throughout the day, unless a dog chases you or maybe a bear. Then it is steady, as are your feet.

Sundays & Weekends

Lord, please give me the strength to get through this upcoming week.

Wonder why yours truly has to go to work on Monday? Mortgage payments? Yes, that's reason number one. Getting away from the obnoxious family is reason number two. What are yours?

Time flies while people watching at the mall. You wonder how all the different people with their different personalities have sex - the serious type, the perfectionist, the introvert, the extrovert, the pervert.

Shopping with the wife over the weekend, buying things you do not need. Bored, you walk the aisles. In the lingerie section, you wonder who fits into some of the larger size bras & panties on display. Just then, you see some voluptuous women walk by, & you eye them with suspicion.

Wouldn't we secretly want every day to be Saturday or Sunday? If only the weekend could be stretched, just a little bit more.

Why isn't there anybody on the streets, in the suburbs, on Sunday evening? Is it football? Or are people sulking about having to go to work on Monday?

Mondays

Early Monday morning, even the toothpaste is reluctant to come out of the tube onto the tooth-brush. Probably it's as sleepy as you are.

The Iphone, the porcelain, & you - as you catch up on emails & happenings around the world. Modern times & the modern replacement of the newspaper! The radio still rocks though.

Driving to work, listening to news, getting bored & switching to music. Switching different radio stations, as you become antsy, switching different lanes on the highway, & finally arriving at work. Wow! What an obstacle course. Now you will have to deal with the people at work.

This one person keeps showing up at every meeting. He got invited because of a typo, but continues to attend; trying to get a word in - to ask why he was invited, but nobody hears him in the very fast-paced meeting. Perhaps he will give up someday, but not today. He may be an idiot, but you cannot doubt his sincerity.

Welcome to Monday & a mad waterfall of things to do for the week.

Work & Corporate America

Remember to suck up to the boss. Repeat mantra three times daily.

Remember to suck up to the leads on your project, the ones who talk a lot at the meetings & have no action items.

Remember to beat up on the weakest links, the ones who are the quietest, have all the action items on the projects, & cannot seem to get anything done. Ever wondered why? Ever wondered why they look so overwhelmed or call in sick so often?

The manager who says, "Let's go & get this project done" one day & the next day, says, "Stop there is another priority," and the cycle repeats. Reminds you of *Godori*, the Korean card game of go-stop.

Ever wondered how some people seem to find it so difficult to follow simple instructions? You wonder if they are not listening, or not understanding.

Taking a walk outside the office, during the lunch break, can be invigorating. The sun actually shines, the birds actually sing & the food outside is so much tastier than the cafeteria.

Why did Susan in Networking get that promotion over everyone else? She must be getting cozy with the boss. The Bitch! Why did John in the PMO get the promotion over everyone else? He must be sleeping with the boss. The Bastard!

Type A personality at work & the Queen Bee syndrome - The world, & definitely the office, ran just fine before you came, & will continue to run, when you are gone. Get a reality check! That pompous air you have around you, is suffocating - the world can do without it & you.

When will telecommuting, be ubiquitous for all commuters? It is after all the closest alternative to teleporting, which is possibly coming in another 100 years?

My dad used to say - "always have a working relationship with everyone at work," even with the most exasperating person. It applies to your personal life as well.

Salary of the highest paid personnel in an organization should be capped, so it does not exceed 20-30 times the salary of the lowest paid personnel. In addition, stock options should be given to all employees. It could be an incentive for the leaders to raise the pay of the lowest paid technician. Don't think that, change in focus away from only profits, will kill productivity, reduce profits, or hamper the quality of deliverables. We can, & do multiple things in our lives. It's time for leaders to do so too.

Sometimes you wonder about people who commute massive distances for work. There should be an option to swap jobs between these extreme commuters or swap homes, spouses & kids.

People commuting for 5 hours - from the Poconos Pennsylvania into NYC? You see them sleeping in the commuter buses, both ways, coming to work & going home. What about the commuters who take the Port Jefferson ferry from Bridgeport, CT to Long Island, NY? Yes, they are sleeping too.

Sometimes you are amazed at how the dirty politics at work, beats that at Washington DC.

The last minute platform change when commuting by train. The humdrum of busy feet reacting to unplanned consequences.

Trains & their ubiquitous delays - Accidents, 100-year old drawbridge not closing, derailment, & now, fire. Still so many basic infrastructure issues, & we are talking about high-speed trains. Can one of the PIGS, perhaps Spain, teach us something here, on how to build and manage infrastructure? Their train system is amazing.

Can anyone multi-task? Perhaps jugglers? Yet, that is the one skill, they say, you need at work.

What is your tipping point? What would infuriate you to quit your job & start your own company or smack the boss or someone else?

Ever forgot to wear your underwear to work or to school? How about the time you forgot to zip up your fly, & the embarrassment that ensued?

It is nice when you see @ssholes get shafted. Let's celebrate. Have a beer.

Office moves & the elaborate preparations & expenditures of the process. Just pick up your stuff,

& go. The phone number can be re-routed, in this day & age of digital communication.

Now we have a term - 'Benefit Corporation'. However, shouldn't we be benefitting from a corporation's presence anyways? Don't we give them enough tax breaks to deserve it?

Sometimes the work-life is circular. You started somewhere, went up the corporate ladder or so you thought & came back to the same place.

Being promoted, demoted, losing your job, & finding another job in the same company, under the garb of doing more with less & creating a flat organization. A weary workout, with a loss of self-esteem in the process!

Movie night with folks at work, followed by a 'constitution' (5 scoops of ice cream) @Port Jefferson, Stony Brook, NY.

Workplace friends to confide in- wishful thinking! Raise your hand if you ever had one or more backbiting co-workers. Time to bite back!

3 PM sugar rush. Bummer! There is no ice cream in the vending machine.

When you were young, there was the teacher's pet, now there is the boss's pet.

Corporate America should value its employees & give them credit. Not just, lip service. Small things matter, like celebrating a job well done. It does not have to be expensive. Not only will an unhappy employee leave, they will also bad-mouth.

Isn't it great, when you get two Kit Kats for the price of one, from the vending machine? You just have to shake the machine a bit harder to make that second one drop. Soda too. Oh these little pleasures of an imperfect world!

McKinseys of the world- Corporate Mafia.

Friday

Lunch at Hooters. Last day at work for John, before he moves to the new job. Good luck dude! Woo hoo! Its work-from-home day. Sumptuous breakfast, long lunch, a few meetings, or hopefully none. Never get your hopes up. You tend to work longer when you work from home, vs. the days you are in the office.

A siesta in the afternoon, after a sumptuous Thai lunch. Wishful thinking.

Drop the clothes at the dry cleaner's & pick them up before Monday. Make sure they fix that broken button & that hole in the pocket of the pant. Ever had your keys fall through the hole in the trouser pocket all the way down your legs? Having second thoughts - Should I have fixed that hole in the pocket of the trouser, myself? $12 could buy half a trouser at least.

Food & Drinks

While watching TV, you wander over to the Food Network channel. Iron Chef, Cutthroat kitchen, Chopped - an abundance of cooking shows & some of them are wild. It is amazing how cooking has evolved over the years & created so many opportunities & jobs!

How many times a week can you eat pizza? Someone I knew had it daily, & was still lean. (Did not check if the toppings were the same). He did play racquetball at lunchtime though.

Ketchup is the new kind of vegetable in the school cafeteria dictionary. Kids love it with fries. Keep on eating, America.

Even Shakespeare would admit that loving food & losing weight are scarce cater-cousins. Keep trying though. Perhaps you will succeed. It is harder with a 24hr Food Network & other such channels. On the flip side, what is the point of living, if you cannot eat a hearty meal?

Spicy Thai food. Spice level: 1 through 5. At 4, your tongue is on fire, & at 5, your rear is on fire. You need that sticky rice with mango dessert to cool off. Please take one portion of it by mouth only.

Day 1 of food at the office cafeteria: So many stations, serving all these incredible cuisines. Awesome place! They know how to feed their employees. Day 30 of food at the office cafeteria: So many stations, serving tasteless hospital-grade food posing as incredible sounding cuisines. Dude, enough of this! Let's check out that new Thai place.

Fast food at MacDonald, Burger King, Arby, Wendy, Jack-in-the-box, Sonic etc. & then there is Rudy's in San Antonio TX. Grilled baby back ribs to die for.

How many times have you binged at a buffet? Are you one of those people who stack their plate with shrimps at the Chinese buffet? Are you the reason, the owners shut shop, & went back to China?

How many beers, before your speech get slurry? Ok, how many Jack Daniels? The quality of the drink speeds up the process. As for Margaritas, two is enough to get you happy & talking stupid.

Stuffing yourself with food leaves you weary & weak. Your movements become sluggish & your brain stops processing information. Yet you will gorge again. Resisting food is futile.

What is the longest you have had to wait to be served at a restaurant? 1 hour? How about at a food truck? Did you checkout the wait times, at the Food Truck Festival, in July of 2014, in North Haven, CT? 1-hour minimum.

Eating at the food trucks. You wonder whether they clean their hands & wash the vegetables. Are the vegetables fresh? But, boy are they tasty!

At a restaurant, you hear the sound of glass & dishes breaking. How often does that happen? Do you pay when you break?

The propensity of frozen yoghurt places, which were in fashion last year, continues to be, this year too - showing no signs of abating. Wonder what the next fad will be?

Sports

Watching Miami Heats vs. San Antonio Spurs, game 5. It's do or die for Lebron James & team. They preferred to die.

Uconn, is rich with basketball money from spectators & alumni. The winner takes it all. It happens when you win both the men & women's national championships in the same year.

World cup soccer nee futball -a sport that could potentially unite the world or divide it. Not too long ago, more people died at this game than at Spanish *encierro*, which has running bulls, & crazy humans in front of them. Nowadays, the futball players bite, & claim, that the inspiration came from a boxing legend.

Nowadays, a 14 years old, cannot head the futball. It is deemed unsafe. Perhaps, they can fist the ball a la 'hand of god', as shown by Maradona in 1984.

US beat Ghana at the soccer world cup - Good. Next, they had to beat the Germans – Not so good.

Brazil & the Soccer, umm..Futball World Cup. Let the demonstrations stop & the games begin, & they did. The game ended with Brazil getting their @ss kicked by Germany. *Guten Tag.*

Germany is celebrating after 24 years. The great German futball machinery – World Soccer champions, 2014.

When you analyze it closely, most sports & games are silly. A Stick & a ball – golf, baseball; 22 people chasing a ball – futball & football. 2 or 4 people hitting a ball/shuttlecock – tennis, table tennis, badminton, & racquetball; 2 people sitting & moving pieces around on a board - chess. However, the money that people make, playing the game professionally, is serious!

Freedom

If you are an employee in corporate America, no matter what your designation is, you are an order taker/executor. Your independence is limited. In other words, you are a puppet.

Do you really have options in life? Are you free? Then why are there controls every step of the way? Why do you need a badge to enter the parking lot & the office?

When you were little, you listened to your parents, a little older, to your teacher, a little more, to your professors. Then you got a job, & listened to the boss. You got a girlfriend, got married, & now you listen to her. Want to have kids & watch them grow? Soon you will be dancing to their tunes too. Oh God! When does this stop? When you die? Then you get to listen to God/Satan. Quite an earful for this lifetime, & beyond!

Need to leave early today. Schools are closing earlier, so have to pick up the kids. Second time this week! What must the folks at work be thinking? Should I login once I reach home & put in an extra hour? Do they actually track the time I am logged into work? With today's technology, it is worse than the punch card days. They know, down to the second, when you logged in, logged out, were away, had lunch etc. You already know that big brother knows all the non-work websites you have been on, how much time you spent there & what you clicked on. Now, if you have a camera on your laptop, they could also know whether you are meditating instead of working or perhaps blinking too many times, adding up to too much shut-eye time on the job.

Why do we feel elated when we are praised & sulk when we feel ignored? Have you ever stopped for a moment, to dwell on it? Bottom line - we are not truly free, & we care about opinions, even though we may want to think we don't.

True Freedom is freedom of thought & of action. How many of us can claim to be truly free?

The pigeonholing continues - black, white, gay, Asian, male, female ... - do we really need to put that on forms? How is this information used? Is it important? I can understand putting blood type, in case you are in an accident, but pigeonholing based on color, caste, & creed needs to go. Not cool, if the strive is for equality.

Pigeon holing people starts with their clothes - what is/ is not the right attire, for which occasion. Pigeonholing can cause a lot of unrest.

Postal workers, plumbers, electricians etc., have uniforms, & the corporate folks have their suits. When it goes beyond, to popes, nuns, & their dress codes, you begin to wonder. Even the bums have a dress code.

Countries & their boundaries! Do air & water have boundaries? How about Music? Can we treat the world as a happy musical place? When do we become citizen of the world, in the true sense?

The Greek musician Yanni & his message of a unified world, accompanied by his orchestra of global musicians - mind blowing & thought provoking.

When will we be color & race blind? When will borders between countries fade?

"Freak" capital - Provincetown, MA? Now, these freaks never stopped you from getting married, so why do you want to control them? Can the same position be taken for abortion?

Awaiting the day, when there will be an international visa, which you can purchase, & travel anywhere in the world. Perhaps the UN can distribute it, they do not seem to be doing much else. This, they can possibly accomplish, & save many people, a lot of hassle - boy, would travel be a charm!

Advice

Do not take favors from others, if you cannot return the favor. You never know when the person you took the favor from, wants his back scratched, & for whatever reason, you cannot return the favor. It could be, that you do not like returning favors, or doing anything for anyone else, besides yourself.

Do not do or say things, which you know you will regret later, & which will tear at your soul (assuming, you have one). Do not do anything that does not make you feel good about yourself. If you lack will power, wean yourself off, gradually.

Rely on your own judgment, not on others.

When you write a derogatory note to someone even though it is confidential, know that it will be circulated. If you must write, at least, make it illegible, & don't sign your name.

Do not speak ill about anyone, on the phone or otherwise. The walls too have ears, especially if, you are in an open cubicle, José.

Reverse mortgage - federally backed! Look closely - In hindsight, would you rather have rented instead of getting into the home ownership game?

When someone is advertising something, is it for your good? Or the advertiser? How many are win – win situations? A few maybe, if you are lucky! Books would be one. Viagra, two. Anymore?

Re-gifting needs some planning. First, you need a tracker of who gave you what, & then, you need to ensure that there is not even a remote possibility, of the past gifter & future giftee, ever crossing paths. Best to re-gift, to a person, in a different city, state, country or a galaxy far far away. This will save you some embarrassment.

Nobody likes to be around a sick person, except perhaps parents, siblings, & close friends. When your colleagues at work looked at you with concern, & suggested you go home & take care of yourself, for a moment, you thought they cared for you. Perhaps you also believed that you were that sincere worker bee in the eyes of all, including the boss. However, what they really mean is – 'keep your germs to yourself'. *Touché!* Truth hurts.

Be active. Inactivity is death. It means you are giving up. You owe it to yourself, not to die yet!

Most people are greedy. There are a very few, truly altruistic people, who will do something good, just for the sake of doing good, & with no other agenda. Which one are you? & who do you want to be?

If you are trying to lose weight, just run. One hour or so, every day. If you cannot run, try walking for an hour. Try it for a month. If it does not work, try watching an hour of TV, daily. Whenever you put in effort for anything, make sure you benefit from it, even if that benefit is some entertainment.

Plan to get life insurance. There are too many morons on the road, trying to kill you. Your loved ones may not love you as much, if they do not benefit from your death.

Technology - accept it. Bigotry - reject it.

Follow your passion. You will be successful & happy. If you do anything else, you will end up a grumpy old man or woman. Either way, my best wishes are with you.

If you are trying to eat right, try eating salads as your meal, for every meal. You will be unhappy but you will lose some of the belly wobble.

If you want to feel good about your weight, hang out with people, fatter than you, or with lower self-esteem than you. Also, recalibrate the scale in your favor (& forget you did it).

Online courses & community colleges are a flexible & cheap alternative to traditional education.

Getting a massage on your neck, back & feet - oh bliss! Stay away from the spas with artificial waterfalls & tranquil music playing from their Bose systems. Checkout the kiosk at the mall, manned by the Chinese. A 10 minute back massage & a 20 minute foot massage @$1/min = Heaven!

Massages are relaxing. Probably as much as, if not more than, sex. Get one weekly, of each, if you can.

Trust a friend more than you would a relative.

How many things do I have to get right, to be successful in life? What is success? Money? Is that it?

Read a story to an underprivileged second or third grader & see how you feel after that.

Statistics, when looked at holistically, tells you an entirely different story, than when you look at it specifically, seeking an answer. You can make numbers speak whatever truth you want.

How many times have you stopped at a traffic light, & when the light turns green, had to honk politely to get someone's attention off his or her phones? Next time, step on the horn.

Entertainers are credited with shaping their times. In reality however, the reverse is probably true. They did entertain well though. There is no need to give them more than their due. No need to follow their lead for everything. Usually, their personal life is messed up. Just do what is good for you. Take ideas & inspirations, but follow your dreams & yours alone. Don't emulate blindly.

Sometimes in life, you have to cut connections. Make sure you cut them cleanly.

Question everything, including anything sensitive.

The truth, if it does not set you free, will at least give you some perspective on what might be going on.

What would make us stop, & question – 'why am I doing, what I am doing?' Answer: - Five Beers.

Work to bring the world together -there is too much dissent, too many fractions, too much fighting.

Make a list of folks you like & those you dislike. Also, add folks you do not care about. Review this list annually.

Let others do what they have to do, but, you should do what you can, in your own small way, to make the world you live in, a better place than it currently is.

Cleanliness, purity, honesty et al, starts with the mind. More specifically, the thoughts in the mind.

Government

Is there any difference between the government, & a large organization? You wonder how anything ever gets done in either place! Take for example, the health care reform implementation in the US, aka Obama care. X year project, X=10, or maybe 20 years... who's counting? A few bones were thrown at you along the way & you are happy.

Student loan repayment has been capped at 10 percent of your monthly income. Nice! However, has it been thought through? Politicians are typically strong on making promises & telling you, what you want to hear, but weak on delivering, & working through the details. Similarly, minimum wage is now $10.10, & the list goes on. This behavior, of politicians sucking up to their constituency, is party agnostic.

Immigrants & immigration - the American cornerstone, & yet we cannot figure out the border issue with Mexico. Somehow, we have figured it out with Canada though. Being poor is a serious curse! Color of your skin, or your English pronunciation, not so much perhaps! Do we really want those people from the south of the border to take over by 2050? *Comprende?*

Kicking the immigration reform past the elections, into December 2014 - that is leadership. Washington continues to amaze.

Immigration to the US in search of opportunities & a better life. Aren't these people in for a shock! Then they made a movie about how America rocks- wonder if the government sponsored some parts of it.

Pork Barrel, big government! I am not going to stand up for all that nonsense. Let me show my displeasure by getting naked & drinking one more beer, this time, with some peanuts & then post on a blog.

If we cannot take care of our veterans, why do we send them to war? Falsifying medical appointments at the VA is quite shameful. Rolling a head will not solve the problem. Fixing the issue at its core is a lot of work. Only way to get it done, is to keep the fickle public interest focused on it.

Greece, the birthplace of Democracy. A show of hand, was all that was needed, to rally people to fight the Persians or for any other decisions, back in 500 BC. Wish democracy was as simple today.

The Fed & their interest rates. They wield amazing power over the stock market & the economy. They exude a yawn, & there are a slew of reporters interpreting that move, & what its likely impact will be on the interest rate.

Edward Snowden's, NSA leaks & taking on the administration did not sit well. Our tax dollars at work, for covert surveillance of us, in the name of national security. When did we sign up for that? Is there an option to opt-out? Why do we have this false sense of security when we know that privacy is just a word? Now, that is a reason to stop paying your taxes, perhaps.

Amazingly, the taxes on lottery tickets, alcohol & cigarettes, fund schools & other public endeavors, as do casinos, bars & brothels in states like Nevada. Does supporting 'good' with the supposedly 'bad' break the bad karma?

Do the homeless have to pay taxes, maybe not property tax? What do they put down as their home address, on their tax returns?

Mortgage backed securities & the search for criminals continues with little success. The problem maybe the fact nobody understands these investments and even less the crimes committed.

Jus Chillin'

(Btw – how are you doing with that beer? Want to switch to a Margarita with salt on the rim?)

Lazing - Sleeping for 17 hours out of the possible 24 is probably the limit. When was the last time you actually lazed with all your might?

Wish you had that amazing house? No, not the ones on HGTV, just a cool house, where lights come on when you clap, the door senses you & opens up, the solar powered garden lights up when you walk out, & you get an alert if you forget to lock the door or close a window when you leave & you can take care of it remotely.

Some restaurants like Chili's, have introduced the concept of placing your order via a touch screen console at your table. You can even swipe your card to pay on it. In addition, while you are waiting, you can play some games on the console for a fee, of course.

More & more people are brewing beer & growing marijuana in their backyard. Pursuit of happiness is a constitutional right. Pursuit of happiness is also an ever evolving, elusive goal.

Wonder what it would be like; if there was no concept of time. No, not just on vacation. Then time flies.

Rants

We complain about the snow in winter & the sun in summer. Instead of complaining the whole time, pick a day of a month to complain. Chill & enjoy life the rest of the days.

Pharmacies need to get their act together on dispensing medicine & on customer service. It is simple. Own the process, make people value you!

The drive-through pharmacy! How many times do you have to spell your last name, remind them you are on express pay, repeat your address, ask if your order went through insurance, be told that they are waiting to hear back from the doctor (could they have called or emailed & saved you a trip?) or had the wrong medicines dispensed. Ironically, you have to rely on them for your medicines. Home delivery? We'll not go there, but do raise your hand, if your insurance company has pestered you to sign up for it.

Sandy Hook, CT. Yes, this could happen in the school your kids go to as well. So, please do whatever you think is right, to prevent it. Do not repent posthumously.

Guns, why are there so many out there? & why is there not enough resistance to limit them? Guns = big business, big business = money, & usually, no one wants to argue with that. Well, some people need to own a rocket launcher, to feel safe.

Crazy people & their crazy guns - you just need either one to go off, to cause ripples in the otherwise humdrum peaceful community life. These days, it seems to be happening every other week.

Taxi drivers - there are good ones & then there are bad ones. Usually, train stations are where you find the bad ones. Check the ones in Bridgeport, CT. You had better negotiate a flat rate for the long obscure ride home or be prepared to be taken for a ride.

You wake up in the morning & get out of bed, with honest intentions of getting things done. You start making a list. By the end of it, you take one look at it & hop back into bed, tired, just from looking at the list.

Ever been to a Laundromat or a parking meter, which accepts only quarters, & realize you are out of quarters? Some say that is how begging started.

Why should I pay for your children's' education, when I don't have any children of my own? A huge chunk of property tax goes towards funding schools. I vote that my money be used for vocational training for all instead.

Why do we give tax breaks to businesses? Give me a break instead.

Flight delays of an hour or so - you sigh, complain, & wait. However, with more delays, comes a point when you say, 'let's just get this over with'. The saga of flight delays & mis-management continues across air carriers.

There are people looking for a handout & there are people willing to give a handout - Each with considerably different motivations. Which one are you?

Globalization or Globalisation

Is globalization spelt with a z or an s? No wonder, we continue to struggle with the concept. How can we unite nations, if we cannot agree on how the word should be spelt?

Bit coin - did you ever understand the concept of software money or digital currency, as some call it? The elusive Satoshi Nakamoto! How many such coins fit in one flash drive?

Current Affairs

Fatwa, Hamas, ISIS, Mullah, Namaaz, Mosque - is some of the news from around the world. Apology, Child Sex Abuse, Gays cannot marry, Pope, Prayer, Church - is the rest of the news.

Spanish princess committing tax fraud! Tough times in Spain with the economic downturn & her allowance being cut, were the driving factors, it is claimed. What next - Spanish princess shoplifting?

Now the Scots want to be "free" from the Brits. Ireland is already free, as are most of the commonwealth nations. What's next? The Catalans in Spain. What really holds us together? Religion?

History? Culture? Economy? Love? Passionate Speech? Fear? Glue?

Freedom was not really for the Scots. They cannot fend for themselves & need to be taken care of. Babies. They would have been free if only they could drink like the Irish, & were believers like them too.

Farming in California equals, fighting for water. Now there are fines for wasting water. What next? It could be drinking re-cycled toilet water, perhaps. Is there value in serenading to the rain gods to end this crisis?

An unstable world with Ukraine, Syria, Iraq, Palestine, Nigeria, Egypt, Sudan, Libya, Afghanistan, Pakistan & the list goes on. Wonder what it takes to stabilize the world...sensible people perhaps, electing sensible leaders. Did that sound like an oxymoron?

Turkey is not a member of the EU. No, it has nothing to do with religion. It is a political & economic alliance. Russia is also not a member. Perhaps there is a hint of sarcasm somewhere.

Putin & the land of Putin- the wild, wild east. Do not mess with the bare crested tiger from Russia. Crimea anyone? *Panimayete.*

Take that Putin! The rout of the ruble – 58 % down this year. Who is the boss now, huh?

Ebola crisis, the plague of the modern times & its impact on Liberia - Reminds you of the plague of the ancient times where people with plague were quarantined & left to die. Horrible tragedy! Now it has even hit home, & killed one person, here in the US.

Sudan has such a rich cultural history, but unfortunately, the wars & other crisis have never stopped since the ancient times. As a result, it continues to be strife ridden, poor & unstable.

Benghazi, Libya has had its history written – a water shed moment in the history of US foreign affairs & the then secretary of state's legacy.

Syria – a beautiful country being destroyed by all the infighting. The United Nations continues to be a defunct organization. Crimea in Ukraine is another such example of a lost cause.

US pour a lot of money into different parts of the world, in the guise of protecting American interest. Nobody votes on these items, at least not the common person. The common American does not give a hoot about the outside world. Mostly it is about protecting the personal interest of those in powers, & not about the country's interest. Look closely at some of the engagements we have around the world.

ISIS (Islamic State of Iraq & Syria) – We will beat you, with our hands tied behind our back. Wonder what happens if they are nimble & change their name to something else in the meantime? Imagine the amount of government documentation across the globe that will need to be updated before going & nixing them. The good thing is, someone, somewhere in the Middle East, is being bombed, for us to feel safer here. Let's Gig'em.

Paris, France & Charlie Hebdo. Finally, the French showed some balls in dealing with terrorism. More nations need to follow suit.

Oh, Israel & Palestine are at it again, as the world watches.

Gaza, Israel & the Iron Dome - finally some protection from the Arabs.

US & Russia with their cold war, & now Syria, Ukraine, Korea, & then there is China & the South China Sea. An ode to power & the need to wield it.

Spain is out of the running for the 2014 world cup soccer championship. The economy was already bad & now this fall from grace.

"Occupy Wall Street" - anybody remember that, from 2011? Nothing came out of it. There was a bunch of people, trying to stroke up a revolution. They are still trying to make a difference.

Crazy border crossing tactics & kids. South America is poor & dangerous. Unfortunately, the problem is spilling over. Amnesty to the illegals! Hmm..For the parents, get in line, behind the legal citizenship seekers.

239 people aboard a Malaysian airline, disappeared, & all efforts & technologies in the world have been unable to find them up to now. Wonder why? What happened to them? Maybe they will show up in a forsaken island, a year from now, hale & hearty. GPS can locate you & your phone down to your exact location. The huge Malaysian plane, however, is another story.

Ukraine or Russia? Wonder who shot the Malaysian plane down. The debate rages on while the international court of justice looks on.

Cuba is an example of a nation, where a pseudo dictator cons its people & its neighbors into believing that they fight for the poor, while free enterprise & human rights are squashed at every pretext. Well, having an embassy in Cuba is going to fix that, or so the President thinks.

How quickly the media's attention switches! What happened to the big oil spill off the Gulf of Mexico in 2010, Boko Haram & the schoolgirls abducted in Nigeria, or David Petraeus & the security breach? The list only seems to keep growing.

Professions & Professionals

Plumbers - if they could only patch the crack of their bottoms, while they fix the cracks in the pipes at the bottom of the sink, the experience would be so much more pleasant.

You hardly ever see a professional cobbler anymore. Wonder what happened…is the cost of repairing shoes & other leather items higher than the cost of buying new ones or are more people just walking barefoot?

Dentistry seems to be a safe profession. Probability of one of your 32 teeth needing attention is high, & you cannot send this job overseas to China or India. You could however, become a dentist, & go to China or India-more people there, so more teeth – more money.

Being a barber, is another safe profession, as long as you target young people, with hair on their head, & balding older people, with hair on their chin. However, the barbers nowadays, rarely give you a shave, they only cut hair. For older people, with hair elsewhere, other than their chin - for that, you need laser hair removal, & that isn't cheap or safe.

Librarians nowadays, need to have multi dimensional interests. They should also be excited about their jobs, & about actively sharing, what they read. I hope that will drive more people to use their local library, more often.

Some people are just not cutout for a customer-facing job. The requirement is simple - smile, & when you have to deliver bad news, apologize, smile some more, deliver the news nicely, apologize again. Whatever you do, don't piss people off. However most of the time, you get exactly the opposite. At the reception of the doctor's office, at the corporate office reception, the railway ticket counter, the airlines check-in desk, or at the car rental pick-up counter - you meet gruff, frowning, easily irritable personalities.

Someone comes up to you & says - "Got some change to spare?", another person says - "Can you give me a dollar?", & a third person says – "Good morning sir," You say -"yes?", He says -"What time is it?". You look at your IPhone & reply - "8:30 am," "Thank you Sir. I am trying to take the train to Brooklyn, & I am short of a few dollars, which I hope you don't mind lending me. If you give me your address, I promise to return it," he says. Which of the three, will you give your money to? Will it change if I told you one of them was wearing a suit?

Wonder who asked Stay-at-home moms to be that? Getting two paychecks is always nicer than getting one, but some people convince themselves, that this is good for their kids. Then proceed to put pressure on the poor husband by asking him to provide this, that & the other. Some stay at home dads behave similarly too.

There are the leaders & there are the followers. Which profession are you in?

Career Advice

Have you noticed, how, most of the songs you hear, have the same lyrics repeated many times over, within the 3 minutes that the song runs. Moreover, if it is a hit, it's worth millions. Best return on investment, if only you could write & sing, & can manage to score a hit. You will be surprised at your fan following, if you can vaguely strum a guitar & move your mouth & say "how do you do." Become a musician if you want to make some serious money, quickly.

Take control of your life, else, someone else will.

Stop for a moment, & take a reality check on your life, & where it is headed - North or South? East or West?

Life is a bitch! Accept it. You are unlucky & will not hit the jackpot or make it to the top of the corporate ladder. Stop buying that lottery ticket & dreaming. Instead, invest that time & money in a business of your own, or in improving your health.

There are two ways to go about getting a promotion or raise at work. One is to kiss-ass big-time, for at least 4 out of the 8 hours in a working day, while hanging out with the boss. And the other, is to continue to do good work, work hard, keep advertising that, & then fight for a promotion. Unless you are in the military or part of a union, these, are the only two approaches that work.

There are some jobs, where sleeping on the job can be an occupational hazard - a night watchman, workers of the third shift at a manufacturing plant, a thief. Yet, it is amazing how all of them do it, & are caught doing so too on social media.

Generally, we are taught to work for others. All schools, colleges, universities, & even the professional courses are geared towards that. Entrepreneurship, building new business, is seldom taught with the emphasis it deserves.

They say it's critical to network, to get a job. How many jobs have you secured through networking?

Money

Ever wonder, how much money, you need to retire? What is your magic number? Start working early on that magic number, within reason. Just do not go overboard. Remember, you also need to eat, pay your rent, & live, even while you save. Don't put all your money into your 401k plan or a ponzi scheme either.

Thinking about the ponzi scheme brought to light by Bernie Madoff, propagated by the media, & incorporated by little made offs on Long Island, NY. Greedy fools & their money are soon parted. How greedy are you?

Debt & the buy now - pay later culture. It exists since ancient times. Back then, you had a debt at the local grocer, because you needed food but did not have the money. Now, it is not for needs, but for wants - a big boat, a big house, big vacations, & big breasts. Afterwards, you can parachute out by declaring bankruptcy & starting the same cycle anew. Bigger boat, bigger house, bigger vacation...need I say more.

How many of our so-called needs can we actually do without? And save that money, to do what we really want. A vacation in Europe perhaps- a visit to Moulin Rouge, in Paris or the Alcazar in Seville.

High rollers & their high life at the casinos! How many of them, do you think are milking the casinos, slowly but surely, while the casinos scratch their heads, trying to figure this out?

Someone hacked into the ATM machine. Why do we need paper money in this day & age? Ah, for that parallel unreported economy. The Feds are coming.

Wonder what the story behind the Swiss & their banks is. Wonder how it all started.

The market crashed, & so did all the indices. Analysts come out & say this, that & the other. If this occurs every 3 or 6 months, you would think the unregulated hedge funds might have something to do with it. You never hear that come up. They are considered a drop in the bucket, but increasingly that drop is getting bigger.

Bartering should cut down the taxes you have to pay on a product, at least partially. I am sure it will be deemed illegal, if it is not so already. I say, go ahead & do it! Let the government figure out how to get more efficient with how they use the money from the reduced taxes, to build whatever infrastructure they need to build.

Banks lend you, your money, at a higher rate. In addition, to get it, you have to have a good credit score, for which, you have to work. Think about that! Look at the interest rate for your checking or savings account at your bank, & then check the mortgage rate or the rate of interest on any other loan, that the same bank offers.

Pet & Kid Owners

Why do dog owners assume that everyone else also loves dogs? It is the same with parents & their kids. That proves, Dogs = Kids.

Why do dog owners keep the leash wrapped around their neck & not on their dogs, when out in public? Look, I know you love your dog, but I don't think your dog loves me! I don't want to be chased by your dog or for that matter have it walking & pooping around me.

A "Thank You" to the parks, which do not allow dogs of any size or shape on their trails. Not even on a leash. Thank you Wolfe Park, Monroe, CT!

Even though you have no children, 60% of your property tax still goes towards funding other people's kid's school education. It is time to take steps, to get even. Have some kids, & have the DINKs & others with homes in your town, contribute towards your kids' education.

Parents will buy anything & everything for their kids. No checks & balances. Does a 3 year old really need an iPad? They are reminded of their own childhood, & probably don't want their kids to suffer from unsatisfied wants, as perhaps they did, growing up in a poor or strict family.

Just watching kids do what they do, can be quite entertaining.

China

Does not matter what you order at a Chinese take-out, it always takes 10-15 minutes. *Ni hao ma.*

The Asian take out is tasty, fast & cheap. Why are people paying so much more for the high-end versions of the same food? For the tablecloth, the prettier crockery or the more fluent English spoken by the server?

There are limited resources in the world & everyone wants a piece of it. China is building Nigeria's infrastructure, roads etc. Wonder why? Not so that, the Nigerians can order cheap Chinese take-out delivered to their doors in 15 mins, for sure.

There is a difference between the Chinese from mainland China, & the Chinese from Taiwan. The ones from Taiwan consider themselves more cultured & sophisticated than the ones from the mainland.

Will the Hong Kong uprising get the Tinnaman Square treatment? Will it sustain? Probably not.

Snow

Cleaning the driveway after a snowstorm, to get rid of 6 inches of snow - Man, what an accomplishment! Makes you wonder, what all that was for. An hour of your life gone just like that. Perhaps the only redeeming feature is, the exercise you got in the process. Thank you Juno 2015.

Why don't the schmucks who plough the streets, raise the plough when they are at the entrance of your driveway? Instead, they deposit everything they cleaned off the street, right at your doorstep! We are taught, defensive driving, when driving cars, how about some defensive snow plowing.

There are many ways to plow the snow. One is to drive your car over it repeatedly, especially if it is too cold, & you do not feel like bundling yourself up in all your snow gear & taking out the snowplow.

Why are electric wires overhead, instead of underground? It's high time underground fiber optic cable was installed, so we are not affected by power outages at the slightest hint of snowstorms. Enough of snow piling on leaves & branches, & the branches crashing down on the electric wires.

Home & Home Ownership

Owning a home - an American dream, or a curse? Why do you need the headache? Is it just to get away from the noisy apartment neighbors, or overbearing property owners or keeping up with the Jones?

The latest fad of listing properties for sale in poetry format is selling fast! There is a sucker born every minute.

Home Depot – As you walk the aisles, you feel your home needs a makeover, & you have the strong urge to buy this & that. If you are really thinking about a makeover - start with yourself, & save some money. Consider all your home projects carefully – & prioritize. They can be serious money pits. You can of course window-shop.

Many years have passed since the housing market's downturn, but you still see homes staying on the market for months, with no buyers. Detroit is going through bankruptcy & having to sell its treasured paintings. Terrible times.

Owning property in the Arctic Circle or Antarctica could be cheap. Heating bill - another story.

Science & Technology & Innovation

Nowadays, there is real coffee on a spaceship. I can understand how that can be a priority, if you are working really long hours in outer space, trying to keep awake, with all that meteor traffic.

Electrical wires that run over the ground should run underground; speed limits should be controlled automatically from within the vehicle or from automated speed monitoring cameras, & the ticket sent home - so many things to fix, to build the perfect world!

When will everything be powered wirelessly?

More fuel-efficient cars would mean lighter cars, & hence, unsafe cars or perhaps a car stripped off air-conditioning & other features! What we need is to be able to thump our chest & say, "energize," just as Capt Kirk used to. It is a cool, cheap,

& fast way to travel. We just need to figure out how the energizer worked in Star Trek.

After more than 30 years, NASA engineers attempt to bring ISEE-3 to life. Good luck.

Drones - humankind's new, automated, war-themed videogame. Civil & military damage, by putting your tax dollars to work, for your surveillance. Drones for Pizza delivery – that, I can support.

How technologies have changed for filling up gas or checking the air pressure. Credit Card vs. Cash only, to pay for the gas. In addition, electric air pumps that sounds an alarm once you reach your target pressure. The nozzle - no change there.

At large parking lots, they should identify & display the spot#s, which are empty, instead of you having to go around in circles, trying to find them. Listen up LaGuardia, NY.

Originally, a meter was not a meter, as we know it today. Crazy people, with crazy concepts of how to define a meter. However, you can blame it on the earth & the need to measure the distance from one spot to another, since ancient times.

Just need to buy eggs, milk, & bread at the grocery store. Eggs - Omega this, farm raised that, cage free, organic, quail eggs, ostrich eggs etc. Milk - 2%, 1%, fat free, vitamin enriched, whole milk etc., & finally, Breads - Rye, white, oat, wheat, whole grain, multi grain, artisan made, seed crusted etc. Wow! I once knew a Chinese person who brought whole milk & added water to make it 2%, & other percentages, as needed.

Motorcycles, mopeds, cars, trucks, trains, bicycles, rickshaws, tractors, or pottery - none of them would have existed, if it weren't for the wheel. That one singular invention revolutionized the world.

Shopping

Have you taken a siesta in the car, while your partner goes shopping at the mall?

Shoes - Nike, New Balance, Adidas, Birkenstock, Steve Madden, Rockport, Bass, Clarks, Cole Haan & so on.
Stocking up on food - Stop & Shop, Big Y, Shoprite, Whole Foods, Traders Joe, Wal-Mart Superstore etc.
Clothes – Banana Republic, Gap, J Crew etc.

Malls - Lord & Taylor, Macy's, Food Court, JCPenny, Target, Cheesecake factory, Victoria's Secret etc.

Electronics - Radio shack, Best Buy.

Wow! The brain is so wired to brands.

Long lines at the checkout counters & not enough stock of merchandize at the stores - no wonder online shopping is growing in popularity.

Women buy clothes & men buy electronics.

Many women do not shy away from buying another purse or another shoe, no matter what the price tag, even though there may be quite a few in their closet already, some even brand new. Emulating Imelda Marcos?

Crime & Craziness

Domestic Violence — Not cool. Period. When a NFL superstar does it, should he lose his job? Whether it is a football star, a movie star or a commoner, beating up girlfriends, wives, or for that matter anyone else, is not cool at all.

Wonder why, more blacks are jailed or are pulled over by the cops. Whether it is Ferguson, Missouri or Staten Island, NY, it continues to play out periodically. Easy with the guns, talk instead.

The number of college rapes should not be shocking. Remember, back when you were in college, & one out of every four men you knew was a jerk, & perhaps capable of rape or molestation! Disassociate yourself from such people immediately. Give no quarter. Don't drink with them.

Bullying, hazing & vandalism are all byproducts of a crowd & the leader of the crowd, both, being out of control. A crowd is a difficult thing to control, as is resisting peer pressure.

Look at all the mass killings & stabbings - one thing is striking…it is usually a man, not a woman, committing the crime. Wonder why?

Kidnapping seems like easy money or is it?

Have you noticed all the various odd places the cops hide, just to give you a ticket? Behind trees, on the grass next to the highway, around blind turns…they hide like criminals! Shouldn't they focus on crimes that are more serious?

To fight corruption & crime - put cameras in every building, & on every street, & make the recordings available to the public real-time.

Now, what about mental crimes? Are you guilty of any? What is the appropriate punishment for that?

If checkout at the grocery store or shopping mall was automated, & there was no one at the cash counter, nor was there any security, would you still pay? What if you noticed that everyone else was walking by with things & not paying? Would you still pay? What's your tipping point?

Wonder what the genesis of organized crime is... Lure of fast cash? Or Lawlessness?

Jails & their inmates - Wonder what it would be like to be in there...not the nice, corporate ones, for the white-collar crimes, but the nasty, real ones, for murderers & rapists. On second thoughts, orange is not my favorite color.

There is graffiti in downtown Ansonia, CT, which reads -"I HATE EVERYONE." The interesting thing is, no one has bothered to remove it. Is that a sign of support or 'whatever'?

Abortion is an interesting question, however, besides the people who are directly involved, everyone else should stay out. None of their business. Murder! You argue.

Texans & their crazy ways - one was printing his own money & had declared Texas an independent country. *Hee- Haw*!

Can a property owner put cameras in the apartment, in the name of security? Not sure, why not? The thought is somewhat creepy though.

Would drug cartels go away, if drugs became legal?

A nuclear Iran – but the question is, why a nuclear any country? Yet, the country, which used those two bombs against Japan, continues to lead in the nuclear arsenal. Fox guarding the hen house.

The only country to drop two bombs on humankind has been the US. It is also a country with a legacy of slavery. Actions will have to speak louder than words, before the world forgets these legacies. Electing a black president is not enough.

The church has done an amazing job of managing its image through the ages, through all the turmoil of the middle ages, & the scandals of today. Corporate Syndicated Church. The mosque however, not so much.

A beggar once refused anything less than a dollar bill. He wanted to have his latte at star bucks.

What should we really do with our lives? Each one's journey is so different. Just don't hang yourself, after having come this far. Go out, be with people, & stop the thoughts, if it ever crosses your mind.

What drives people to commit suicide? Probably they take life a little too seriously. Perhaps watching an hour of John Stewart on Comedy Central daily should be the prescribed therapy.

The cops at Arizona State University brutally arrested a professor for jaywalking. Never mess with authority & never mess with your students. They will give you a bad evaluation. Why the cops don't have evaluations, you wonder.

All public officials, including cops, should have their records available online for all to see, "like," & post comments on, similar to Facebook.

Murders, stabbings, shootings – all mostly committed by men. However, you wonder, who instigated them?

Murderers, whatever their motive, will not change. People do not change. They may change their appearance & what comes out of their mouth though. Take yourself for instance...has the basic "you" changed?

How safe do you feel in your own home, when a random man is able to jump over the fence of the White House? Julia Pierson resigned over the matter. Who is going to resign if this was to happen to you? Your home security system?

Why are all Evelyn Brother's, songs, always about lost love & prison, & no other sentiments?

Relatives

Mom – Unbalanced love
Dad – Balanced love
Grandma & Grandpa – Unconditional love.
Wife – Not saying 'I love you' is hazardous.
Girlfriend – Hap-hazard, murderous love
Husband – What is love? Give me the TV remote.

Boyfriend – Cut the love talk baby. Let's make-out.

Son – Wonder what he will grow up to be.

Daughter – You worry about her more than you worry about the son.

First Cousins – Laugh, eat, drink & hangout

Son & husband – He's mine (mother's, wife's)

Mother-in-law – When will she leave?

Daughter-in-law – Not good enough for my son.

Father-in-law – Now that is a nice man.

Relatives can be nosey creatures. They want to know everything that is going on in your life. Humor them with the wrong information.

Houseguests - The good ones leave in a day or two, but then there are the ones, who are like the heat wave in July, you eagerly await their departure.

When you think about loved ones, & other people you knew, who are no longer there, your emotions are rarely grey, - they are either really good or really bad.

Doctors, Hospitals, & Such

$350 for a consultation with the doc. Rip off or totally, worth it, you decide.

They speak glibly, are well dressed & handsome, & you wonder - 'am I paying for that gel, that hairdo, that monogrammed shirt?'

Seems that the only good doctors are in the walk-in urgent care centers. They are the ones getting the experience from the widest cross-section of patients, with all their interesting ailments. They truly rock! The others, mostly, hide behind the garb of specialization. We need more of the former breed.

You have a tooth problem, so you need a dentist. However, do you need an endodontic, periodontal, prosthodontic or a general dentist? I bet you thought setting-up this appointment would be easy.

AIDS, cancer, diabetes, high blood pressure, common cough, & cold - do we have a cure for any? Will we ever have a cure for the root cause of any ailments or continue to do patchwork by treating the symptoms?

Prosthetic limbs, artificial heart, liver transplant, bone marrow transplant etc....oh, & Plastic surgery - It is amazing what the doctors can do these days to improve our longevity & quality of life.

Co-pay, co-insurance, out-of-pocket maximum etc. - & all you wanted was to have your health issue fixed.

Look at your health insurance card, & if you understand all of it, pay yourself $20 in co-pay. You, my friend, are an enlightened one!

For those who are not so evolved, here are some of the other things you may see – coinsurance, in/out network, primary care, specialist, hospital, ER, urgent care, & Rx group. Is your head swimming? Ready to give up? Relax, have a drink my friend.

For those, who do not have a health insurance card, ignorance is indeed bliss. Stay that way. What you don't know can't hurt.

Waiting at the reception of the doctor's office, while the receptionist is pushing paper. Wonder what the doctor is busy with? Another patient? Hot nurse? Reading your file to remind him who you are? Wonder why they can never keep time? Why is their writing invariably illegible, with potentially terrible consequences on the medicines you swallow? Yet, we trust them blindly.

Waiting for the day when doctors' clinics are open round the clock, for you to go to whenever you are unwell. No, not just the ERs at the hospitals. There are 24-hour McDonald & Wal-Mart. Why not a doctor's clinic? When did chicken nuggets & laundry detergents become more important than your fever or toothache?

At the doctor's office or the hospitals, consider the amount of time you spend waiting. You wait at the lobby, then the nurse kills some time checking your weight, height, blood pressure etc. (none of which is related to the ailment you are there for), then you are taken to another room to wait for the doctor. Finally, when the doctor does come in, he asks you to change into the paper gown & goes away again (so why did the nurse not tell you that?). Almost like Disneyland, & the wait time to see your favorite character or get on your favorite ride.

You spend a third of your life sleeping & a fourth of your life waiting. You wait for your girlfriend to show up. At work, you wait to get coffee, you wait at the cafeteria register, & you wait for someone to finish his or her part in a project, before you can start yours. The worst wait however, is the wait for someone to get out of the bathroom, so you can get your small or big act going.

Oh, for a world where all your physicians, including your primary care, specialists, & dentist, talked to each other & knew exactly what was going on with you? A social media of the anatomy is the need of the hour. Imagine the status updates - the likes and dislikes on posts!

Drug related deaths at Martha's Vineyard - Medical marijuana made legal, without the implementation of checks & balance.

Politicians & Lawyers

Wonder why most politicians are lawyers.

Members of the house & senate make $174,000 per year, majority, & minority leaders -$193,000, cabinet members - $199,700, the speaker - $223,500, the Vice President - $230,700, & The President - $400,000. Average household income in the country - less than $55,000.

I vote for, politician's pay being the same as, the average pay of all the Joes & Janes in the constituencies they serve.

Politicians deceive us repeatedly, & still, we never learn.

Why do public officials take up those positions? Power? Money? Ability to bully?

The State of the Union address was like watching a feel-good movie, with the feelings lasting a week or as long as the media wanted us to feel it, & then, on to the next bright & shining object. Sometimes you wonder who has the controls. The media or the people?

Why are there so many props at the State of the Union address? Each prop speaks more than a thousand words perhaps! Moreover, the national & international audience is rather stupid. They need the props to understand the complex work being done, by the government. These props are the Microsoft Power Point slides of the state of the union address.

Once elected, most politicians lose touch with their constituents. Cya in another 4 years, or 2, if you are really lucky!

A Vice President, who can talk your ears off - What is it with old men & sailors?

Tigers & lions & bears, oh my! Judges & lawyers & politicians, oh my!

Yes, Hillary is going to run to be the next President. Why? Because, she wrote a book, just like President Obama. However, she probably will not be able to win. Too much baggage, not enough charisma. Some people crave the power to lead & change the world.

$250,000 for speaking to students at UCONN, CT. Hillary seems to be raking it in, after claiming to having gone broke, after leaving the White House. She claims to understand what the poor go through. Hello? Give us a break! Hard choices indeed!

Will Obama Care rescue the healthcare costs or add to it? It appears to be a mixed bag, leaning towards adding costs. Removing the word "affordable" from 'the affordable care act' might make sense. There was the healthcare.gov website fiasco & now there is an Obamacare 2.0. Folks, better start running - for your health, I mean.

Politics - the golden path for money & power, the two ingredients, that you think, will make you happy.

Policy & Politicians are like north poles of two magnets. Nine out of ten decisions by a politician are motivated by a political agenda, rather than a firm thought through position on a policy.

Why do we pay our politicians? Let the bureaucrats handle it all. It is a waste of money.

Now casinos in Massachusetts & Pennsylvania are in competition for your money. Public policy at play.

In the last few wars that have been waged, wonder how many kids of senators & congress members have been defending the country? Let the leaders lead by example & get some skin in the game, be the first to have their kin sign up, when we go to war.

Republicans & Democrats are two sides of the same fake coin. Choose the lesser of the two evils, or choose the third option. Most likely, neither has done anything, recently, to make a difference in your life. Do not suddenly become optimistic for the future. Treat them just as you would treat the stripper who takes you to a destination, nothing more, nothing less. Good service – dollar on her G-String, bad service - dollar off her G-String.

While the common person struggles in their daily life, with putting food on the table, due to the ever-increasing cost of essentials like milk, bread & other groceries, there are folks in Washington figuring out who should be the next majority leader, over a fancy white- tablecloth dinner.

Sometimes you can't help but wonder, who oversees, a political decision which over-rides a well-vetted technical decision.

Can taxation be considered an extortion or ponzi scheme? You pay, they collect, they distribute, they even control the interest rates on returns ...think hard. What about social security?

Public funding of local candidates at $1 MM for the primary & $5 MM for general election - the numbers are overwhelming! To think you could retire, if you had $5 MM. The amount of money that is blown away at local elections is overwhelming, & to what end? Is your life any different since the last election? So, why are you cheering for these candidates?

Students cramming before their exams or the Congress's last minute efforts to keep the government open at the end of the year...Priorities!

Airlines, Airports & Aircrafts

Who sized & designed the airplane potty? Wonder if that person ever used it. Time to flush it.

The airlines continue their cheap tactics. Pay for checking in luggage, for sitting together, for your food. What next- $10 to use the restroom Hold that thought, I mean hold that pee.

Airline seats are getting more cramped. Not sure what the goal is. If it is to entice people to upgrade to Business class, it's not happening. It's just pissing people off. Next time, if they can, they will sit on the wings or drive to their destination. It's a wakeup call for potential lost business.

In the men's rooms of terminal 4 at JFK, there is a picture of a fly, that seems to move, you have to aim for. Peeing has never been so much fun!

Airport drop-off areas, with their honking taxis. Irritating. Peace & Patience is the call of the hour.

The amount of luggage people check-in is so varied – ranges from six matching LV suitcases between two people, just because you are flying business class, & are entitled to it, to the light travelers with one back pack for an entire month in Europe. Wonder what is packed in those six suitcases - bras, panties, thongs, handcuffs, shoes, makeup!

Air Traffic Safety! How many bird & plane accidents have we had, since the Wilber brothers flew at Kitty Hawk or Gustave Whitehead flew his plane over Bridgeport? Who was not looking, the bird, or the pilots?

Flying aircrafts - small & large. Small ones feel like driving a car, look to the left, look to the right, look to the left again, & off you go, except you are taking off into the air. They also need a much shorter runway, compared to the Boeing 777.

Holidays & Vacation

Key West – the cigars are good, as is the *cortadito* - double espresso shots with sugar & a wee bit of milk. Heaven in a cup!

Pitter-patter of the rain, lush green trees, chirping birds, lazy morning with a cup of coffee. Bliss!

Romance on a lake, with the lazy slurping of the oars on the water, creating melodious, lilting musical lyrics of a love song, as the moonlight shimmers through.

Early mornings with chirping birds, soft rain & the fresh smell of the damp earth - the simple things that make life worth living. Mornings can be very invigorating.

Watching 12 movies in a week, over the Christmas break, has to be some sort of record.

A man is dumpster diving at the airport - why, you ask? Bum is hoping to get a ticket to visit Singapore, with a stopover in Japan.

Interestingly, anything Greek, was accomplished between 500 BC & 0 AD. After that, it was the Romans & the Turks. Talk about living off past glory.

Sifnos, Mykonos, Paros, Naxos, Milos, Ios, Syros, Amorgos, Andros, Antimilos, Antiparos, Delos, Folegandros, Kimolos & the list goes on, of the rhyming Cycladic islands.

White & Blue Santorini - wonder who has the colors contracted out with the local administration.

Sifnos, with its churches, cliffs makes for unbelievable landscapes.

Lapping of the waves, the hopping & bleating of the mountain goats, the incessant chirping of the birds, the soft breeze, the contours of the terrain, tall hills, & paved walkway - quaint, lovely, beautiful, Kamares village, in Sifnos, Greece.

Vathi, a sleepy village in Sifnos, Greece. Sandy beach bay, tall hills.

Ornate chimney tops, local artisans making pottery & chick pea soup on Sunday, that sums up the island of Sifnos, Greece.

In Athens - strolling the Acropolis & Temple of Zeus, makes you feel like you are walking in the past & present simultaneously. You realize that the world is complex, & that everything that has happened, past & present, needs to be embraced.

As the story goes, Hawaii has its chicken & Greece has its cats.

Whether you go to the forest or the beach, have a good time whenever you can, wherever you are. It will lift up your spirits.

Whom do the turkeys thank for Thanksgiving? The President of the United States, that's who.

Is the day after Thanksgiving a holiday, to help us recover from over eating? Or to help us shop?

Pebbles in the water of life. Each, to step on, to reach that mountain out there yonder.

Jackson, a small quaint town in New Hampshire has an annual ritualistic yellow-rubber-duck race — cute!

Beautiful New Hampshire with its mountains & streams - nature's paradise.

Wonder what the beach, the water, the mountains, & the sky say to each other when they meet at the horizon.

Wouldn't it be wonderful to lie in bed, inside a room made of tinted glass, including the roof & the floor, where you can look out, but nobody can look in. Sounds cool. Now somebody needs to build it.

Bubbling hot mud springs & the hydrothermal wonders of nature - Lassen Volcanic National Park, California.

Yosemite National Forest, California - Interesting contours in the landscape.

House boats & coconut trees in the lapping backwaters of Kerala, India.

Roads & Cars & Driving

Did NASCAR derive its name from 'nice car'?

A car dealer once told me that, he has been servicing a green 1987 Honda Accord with 687,000 miles on it. Eventually, even though everything else wore off, the engine was still good. Wonder what the story is with the other cars & their gear train warranty? In the long run, everything will fall off; including the steering wheel, but your gears will work. Consider the car where everything else falls off and you are left holding the steering wheel.

Death due to ignition switch failures in cars, continues to be discussed & investigated. Amongst all the other items being pursued, when was the last time the government body NHTSA, recalled a vehicle, unilaterally?

Ever been in a small car, sandwiched between two 18-wheelers, on a 3-lane highway? Those should only be driven on parkways, where no trucks are allowed. Why ride with the big bullies.

Driving to work & listening to CNN, FOX, switching to some local news, then to NPR - Thanks to the new car with free Sirius subscription for 6 months. (Will have to check the papers to confirm). David Bouchier's humor reminds me of P.G. Wodehouse.

Potholes, the after effects of a horrible winter, make for an off-the-grid driving experience.

Are the craziest drivers out only on Friday nights? I thought, alcohol either put you to sleep or made you happy, either way you stayed home.

While driving on the highway, you remember lost relations, an event, a place, a person – something re-kindles those sweet memories & tugs at your heart.

A bunch of yellow wild flowers by the roadside, beautiful.

Detours & evacuation signs, following them can be quite daunting.

I have seen a number of cars on fire, while driving on the highways. I distinctly remember one, at a tollbooth on NJ Turnpike, & another, on RT 8

North, near Waterbury, Connecticut. Wonder how these fires happen?

Ever rear-end someone, while searching for quarters, as you were approaching a tollbooth? Do you have that EZ Pass yet?

A tractor-trailer lay toppled on the highway. Wonder what could have made that whale of a vehicle tank down sideways. $F = MV^2/R$.

Covered bridges are a delight to watch, as you drive through the New England countryside.

Driving through the hills, & valleys, with the wonderful fresh air & the lazy brook gurgling along on the side. A small cute little bridge called the 'kissing bridge', in the beautiful Connecticut countryside.

What is the most interesting license plate you have seen? Can you beat *'Cops lie'*?

A truck without the trailer, somehow, looks like a big face with no body or reminds you of a dachshund, the dog with short legs.

Driving down the Henry Hudson parkway in NYC, is quite exhilarating, as you watch the interesting buildings on the left, & the river & New Jersey on your right, until you hit the first traffic light. Then, it's mayhem.

There are street lamps on some parts of the highway & then you don't see them anymore. Why do you need them anyway? Are your car headlights not functioning?

At a four-way stop sign, you wonder why there are so many French people in USA, waving their hands to give you the right of way. Americans are more polite than the French.

Good luck finding parking at train stations in the suburbs of New York. If you are planning to commute by train, know that, some of the parking lots, have a wait period of several years.

Old Connecticut towns like Derby seem quaint, until you spot the old rotten cast iron bridges, which could collapse any day.

What goes on in your mind, when you are backing up your car on a busy street & your Mini Cooper is parked between two Ford Explorers? Will I live or die?

How it is that you are invariably stuck behind a school bus, on a single lane street, when you are rushing to get to work. Even the bus driver is sympathetic.

When you need a restroom break really badly, do you prefer a service area alongside the highway, rather than taking an exit & risking getting lost?

When driving to work - which is the right lane to stay in? What about when driving back home? Is the left lane the right lane to stay in?

What was the longest you were ever stuck in traffic? How did you manage pee-pee? Did you wear space diapers as one astronaut did in her travels to Florida several years ago?

We drive our cars around so much! Going to work, going for groceries, going for a movie, or to buy clothes, or for a meal with friends, driving the kids to soccer practice, an occasional road trip…& on & on it goes. A reliable friend, Monty.

Solution to traffic problems - Let everyone work from home or walk to work.

Yellow lines, white lines, single lines, lines with dashes & then the double lines on the streets. A

Martian or an alien would have a tough time navigating our roads. One got lost trying to get to DC to open lines of communications.

Aren't you amazed at the brands of cars on the road? Benz, BMW, Toyota, Honda, Isuzu, Subaru, Chrysler, Ford, General Motors, Kia, Hyundai, Tesla, Volkswagen, & the list goes on.

As you drive, you see the different types of cars, different sizes, different colors, different brands & then there are other types of vehicles. Amazing variety of vehicles - Big trucks, regular sedans, SUVs, RVs, funky convertibles, sporty motorcycles, expensive Bugattis, & even some classy vintages. What would the net worth of the highway be?

As you pass by the exits on the highway, you see exit 16, exit 17 & then exit 19. What happened to 18? Either exits are mile based or they are consecutive. What is the story here?

Perpetual dilemma - You are in the exit lane, but do not want to take this exit, & there is this huge truck next to you, on your left. Do you speed up or slow down?

Given a choice between sharing the road with cement mixers, dump truck or school buses -vote for the relatively faster school buses. In addition, if the choice is between donkeys & horses, if you happen to be in a third world country or in Texas - go with the horses.

Trucks keep getting stuck under the bridges on the Merritt parkway. Mr. Truck driver - there is a reason there are signs all over telling you about the height of the underpass & there is a reason why, you are not allowed on the parkway. Idiot.

Have you ever skidded on black ice & found yourself facing traffic? Scary! Take my word for it.

Sunshine in your face on your drive to work & some more, on the drive back home. Can be rather irritating, when you cannot see where you are going, & a part of you is betting whether you will rear-end someone or someone will rear-end you.

Driving back & forth from work, you wonder how you make it, having to watch out constantly for all those crazies, who are causing countless accidents every day. Without your defensive driving skills, & your driving swagger, you would be toast.

Have you ever been in a speed trap? When Officer Goon walks over with that smug expression, what do you do? Show him the finger & take off? You wish. Some women show cleavage & legs to get away.

Have you ever jumped a red light? How many times have you wanted to? How many times have you been caught doing so?

What is your best excuse for a speeding ticket? "Give me a break officer, a ticket for going 31 on a 25? I can't even brag to my friends about that!"

The jackass, who cut you off on the highway, ran into a guardrail & his car caught fire.

Have you ever seen a moose hit a car or the other way around? Travelled to Maine & NH to see if things like that actually happen, with not much luck. Why the tempting road signs then?

While picking up your medicines from the drive-through pharmacy, you are behind a car, which has not moved for the last 15 minutes. Do you keep waiting, can't be much longer after all, or do you turn around & leave, hoping that tomorrow you will be luckier?

Driving along Roosevelt Avenue in Queens, NY - gives you a taste of the world. Each block is a country - Columbia, Peru, China, Thailand, Guatemala, Mexico, El Salvador, Korea, Vietnam, India, Bangladesh, Nepal, & some that you may not have even have heard of....

You see trucks on the road, & wonder about where they are coming from & where they are headed. Even though they are the best drivers on the road, they still carry a sign asking you to call an 800 number to complain, if you have concerns with their driving. You would think some cars & motorcycles should be carrying that sign too.

The perils of driving on the road are increasing. The gradient on the roads are getting steeper, turns sharper, crazy merge signs & going downhill, is a roller coaster ride. It's time to trust a search engine to drive your car.

The never-ending saga of road construction! Rough patches on the road for 2 months! When will it get fixed? Heard there were budget cuts. Wonder who funds the roads & its upkeep? Now there is talk of tolls for all the roads. Wonder where all your Fuel surcharge & tax dollars went. Are they being used for wars? Or for filling the pockets of bureaucrats & politicians?

Why do we pay tolls? Aren't the taxes enough – from the various State, Fed, City, County taxes? Sometimes you feel that you go to work for everyone else, but yourself, & the intensity of the feeling depends on your tax bracket.

New York has the most expensive tolls. The toll on the Whitestone Bridge is $7.50 & the George Washington Bridge is around $13. The Verrazano takes the cake at $15. Compare these with a city like Chicago, where the tolls are $1 or $2.

You have seen police officers on foot, on a bicycle, a motorcycle, a horse, a car, in an aircraft, in a chopper & on a boat. How about a truck?

We now have an un-patented electric car - Tesla. Wonder what it will trigger - more cars that are electric?

Driving on the other side of the street in Great Britain, takes some getting used to, especially when the steering wheel is also on the other side.

How many times have you floored the gas pedal in your car & rocketed off, with no cares in the world? Remember the feeling? Next time, just do it at the racetracks.

While driving, voices you hear during the day play in your mind. Some stick & go on auto play.

The Sexes & Relationships

Women - Manipulative bitches. I rest my case.
Men - Lazy bastards. I drink to that.
Gays & Lesbians – Now you are married. Now you are not. Now it is legal. Now it is not.

Are all the hot girls in Human Resources? And all the hot men in the construction business? Wonder where they will go when these professions get outsourced.

For women, looking good, is time consuming & expensive. Haircut, keratin treatment, hair color, mineral pedicures, french manicures, facials, waxing of the arms, legs, upper lip & some other parts of the body, bronzing, Botox etc. Not so for the men. Granted, most men are not trying to look pretty.

Not all men are handsome & not all women are beautiful. That explains the fan following for those elusive people that walk this planet.

Body odor - men do not care as much, women do - sniff, sniff.

Why can women wear almost anything to work, while men are tied to their khakis? The hemlines keep getting shorter every progressive summer & flip-flops have replaced sandals.

Summer brings with it, the need for some women to wear short dresses & raise the general temperature. Global warming!

Single people, married people, & people who are married, with kids - should all be given the same civil & tax benefits. It may stop some from getting married for the wrong reasons!

In this electronic age, patience is a rare commodity, especially in relationships.

Sometimes you feel that, you are the one doing everything around the house. The other person does nothing. Actually, you always feel that way. It's called justifying your contributions & it is not necessarily the truth.

Women want to talk about their problems & work through them. Most men do not. For women it's about feeling bad, then expressing that, & then finding closure by having a conversation about those feelings, perhaps followed by a hug.

While men are sitting there thinking - why are we having a conversation about feelings?

Women & men are just wired differently. Let us not waste any time trying to fix that.

It is no longer a man's world. Was it ever, really?

Wonder why women go to pee, in a group. Togetherness should be limited. The next thing would probably be sharing a stall. The Japanese or the Germans may even have designed something by now.

Behind every divorce, there is usually an affair. The trigger however, could have been a multitude of things – mostly stemming from, not being happy in the relationship & a need to change it. Finance is a leading cause but I think it is snoring. Man or Woman, you need a good night sleep & not be cranky when you wake up!

Cheating spouses have been around since Adam & Eve. Yet, we are shocked when it happens to us or around us. Given the opportunity, people will cheat & steal, as long as there are no consequences & no conscience.

Clark Gable was married 5 times in his 60 years.

Many other celebrities have had multiple marriages. Does the number of Marriages tell us something about their personality? Does this go back to the question of having the opportunity & there being no consequences? There is always that first step, for that next marriage to happen.

People divorce, marry, & divorce again. Does this mean they believe in the institution, but not in the institutionalized partner, or that they never learn.

The quest for "better," prompts change, & is never satisfied - change of car, change of house, change of job, change of friends & change of spouse. Some do it once or maybe twice, while others do it several times.

Trying to find love online? Whatever happened to old fashion dating? A computer program to match you on various categories with your chosen one. Really? It's hard enough to find a house online! Do you really need that much help from a computer in your life?

Love is overrated! Wonder who marketed it first. Romeo or Juliet? Thanks for creating this billion-dollar, valentine day phenomenon. Not complaining though, anything that creates jobs is good. I am all for the economics of love.

When did Valentine's day, Mother's day, Father's day all become major national festivals?

Love between two adults - is an overrated feeling. It comes & goes.

Love is a crazy thing. It makes people do crazy things, which they regret later or smile smugly about when they remember it.

Marriages were not made in heaven. Someone came up with the idea, some others thought it was nice, & the craze caught on.

Why do people marry? What percentage is for love? Primarily, it is because of financial security, parental pressure, peer pressure, lure of fame by association, resume value of the spouse, promise of a good lifestyle etc. Where does love figure amongst the priorities?

Celebrities, Movies & Entertainment

Movies & popcorn! It's amazing how people go for "free refills" on the large popcorn tubs. Did they bring along their neighbors & feeding them too?

Do you know what Ricky Martin's citizenship is? Does it really matter when he is shaking his bon-bon in Spain?

Who is this Shakira? What do her hips have that other women do not? Well, they shake, & they don't lie!

The Oscars prove that college degrees are not necessary, for success, in the field of acting.

Who is the most famous person that you have met? Bet you, 9 out of 10, they were not as cool as you thought they would be.

As you flip through the TV channels, you wonder if the cable company took you for a ride - did you really pay for all this.

'Twelve years a slave' is a movie that can shake your world, if you are watching closely. We owe a lot to the black man, having prospered at his cost. This history of America is not pretty, & we need to recognize that.

'Twelve years a slave' also makes you think about how some businesses continue to enslave (even if it is indirectly, in some far off nation, in the name of globalization), pay poor wages & have poor working conditions - all for maximizing their profits. Earlier, it was the cotton. Now, it is cheap clothes, shoes & electronic items.

Judi Dench delivers a great performance in Philomena. What does age have to do with performance?

If you get bored with *'Dancing with the stars'*, watch *'Strictly come Dancing'* – its where the show gets its inspiration. The original is phenomenal.

So many dance moves - Cha-Cha, Foxtrot, Rumba, Jive, Swing, Waltz, Hustle, Salsa, Merengue, Tango, Ballet, Tap, Line dancing, Pole Dancing & then, of course, there is freestyle. How many can you swing to?

Kim Kardashian & social media. Social media seems to have a bias towards women, since they tend to have curves that men lack. In addition, they can talk glibly, another thing most men lack (sailors excluded). People, let's even the playing field & give them some tax breaks to get some curves & tongue. This is your President speaking.

Oh, the TV shows - Everybody loves Raymond, Seinfeld, Married with children, Friends, The big bang theory, Lente loco, 12 Corazones, & the list goes on. Watching re-runs to while away time. Wonder if people would be couch potatoes, if the shows were not so engaging & interesting... Is bad television programming, good for health?

The Big Bang Theory is quite a funny show. Wonder what those characters are like, in real life. Are they as weird?

Marketplace, on NPR is informative and fun, but without Kai Ryssdal – it sucks! No sick day or vacation day for him.

Why do some of us watch reality shows, so eagerly? Is it the age-old phenomenon of deriving amusement at the expense of other people?

Reality TV - Big Brother, Bachelor, Bachelorette, Jerry Springer etc. Oh yes, there are so many of us, who, secretly want to watch, the bizarre things that other people are doing. Nothing else, would explain, the sustained high ratings of these shows.

Comic book characters, are such an integral part of your life, growing up. The Archie's, Batman, Superman, Flash Gordon, Wonder woman, Axa, TinTin, Asterix & so on.

What were the superheroes thinking, when they decided to wear their underwear over their clothes? Too constrained in here.

American Ninja warrior motivates you to watch more TV. Amazing folks, with amazing determination & ability.

Comedians & standup comics - There are so many of them, but only a few are funny & can keep their jokes clean. Gabriel Iglesias aka Fluffy, is one such, who comes to mind.

These days, promotions for movies are so blatant, with the actors doing the rounds at various popular talk shows, & other cookie-cutter options, which all of them seem to follow. Wish the focus was, as much, on the quality. So few good movies are being made. Just make a good movie that I can watch & enjoy – don't bother about fitting it into a genre label.

In NYC, expect to bump into celebrities, walking down the street, who are not expecting to bump into you.

Too much credit for melodious music goes to the singer. The lyricist, the music director, the accompanying musicians should get the real credit.

Next time you hear a great song, do find out who those people behind the scene are, & thank them.

Love songs reflect their times. "Lipstick on your collar" has this rather cheery "yeah" in it - which makes you wonder - are you happy or sad girl? Songs - during periods of high inflation & high unemployment, grovel & lament. In happier times, they are more upbeat, perhaps about having found a better boyfriend or girlfriend... & then, there are the ones, which are timeless. Think, John Denver's "you fill up my senses."

An amazing number of people grace the casinos everywhere. Let's see - good shows, good food, un-limited alcohol, scantily clad women & the potential that all that, will be paid for, by the money you may win.

How a simple instrument creates such beautiful & melodious music - the flute.

Movies & movie stars - so much money to be made, by selling dreams to the common person.

Religion

Interestingly, we continue to believe in the oldest religions & seem to have believed in them for generations, like zealots. However, yesterday's technology is old today. Talk about double standards. How often does religion get an OS upgrade?

We listen to the God men & other such people, & do as they tell us - ever wonder why? They have the gift of the gab, they tell us what we want to hear, play to our fears, & are well dressed too. They come very well prepared, for their interview with you.

People continue to be ignorant & superstitious. Not knowing the unknown seems to be at the core of it, & some coincidences, falsely credited to being cause & effect. I crossed my fingers, & the plane I was travelling in, did not crash. Let me cross it again, as I trek through Gaza in the Middle East propagating peace & love, & no bullet will hit me.

Judaism, Islam, Hinduism, Christianity, Buddhism, Paganism, Baha'i ... the list of religions in the world, is long. Ironically, most talk about the notion of - "one God". The quest for finding a religion that fulfils you & your beliefs is purely a personal journey.

Religion based militancy arose long before the formation of Al-Qaida or ISIS (Islamic State of

Iraq & Syria). Back in the middle ages, the pope ordered it. Payback time? Christianity & Islam - the two religions that have a history of the most bloodshed, perhaps because they have tried to convert, unlike the others, like Buddhism. Religion is your personal equation with God. Why bring anyone or anything in between - Popes, Prophets, Priests, Rabbi, & such. Have they seen God!

The similarities are striking; Christians have Protestants & Catholics, Muslims have Shia & Sunni.

The Sistine Capella - a chapel where one of the most powerful leaders of the religious world is announced. That one person, along with the institution, has done some good & much bad over the centuries, including now. The imams and the caliphate are following suit.

Sisters, Fathers & the missionary system - Why does religion have to be so organized, unless, it is a business? Why does the church, or anyone else, have an influence over your relationship with the almighty? Interestingly, none of them has actually seen the almighty, but speak glibly on the subject. Same goes for the other religious leaders.

Do not know of anyone, personally, who saw the white light on the other side & came back a changed person. Wonder why, that light was white, & not neon & jazzy, like at the nightclub. Oh! Those neon & jazzy lights are from hell. I mean, you may want to do good & still want to end up in hell - I am told its cooler.

Nudity

Only if you are good looking. I have my rights too - I refuse to see fat & ugly nude people.

You can sunbathe & I can watch.

How we have managed to make our lives so busy! Travel to work far away, stop at the post office on the way , pick up groceries on the way back, with a stop at the mall too, tending the garden, cleaning the house, throwing the trash, making dinner, doing laundry ... was everything important? What do you really need to do? Perhaps the vagabond nudist has figured it all out & has a perspective on life that we can learn from.

Life

What do you really need to live? It started with air, water, food, shelter, & clothes. Enter Money. Anything else? Love maybe?

Love & Air - the only commodities, which are free? Enter Valentine's Day - Chocolates, flowers, gifts, & cards for the women. Men get the honor of providing and being rewarded with a kiss on the cheek and some boom-boom shaka-laka later.

What is the most bizarre thing you have done in your life? Stopped the moving ceiling fan with your hand! How old were you when you did it? Would you do it again?

Why do we support a cause? Is it because we truly believe in it? Or because of peer pressure or because we need something to feel good about?

Life is interesting. It is hard to be an optimist, when there is so much pessimism around you. When people pull you down, all they are trying to do is, get ahead of you. There is only so much food on the table. It is after all, survival of the fittest. Moreover, it gets worse, in third world countries & New York City – with many more people fighting for fewer resources.

Try to remember, five good things that have happened to you, in your life. Now, think of five bad ones. Most likely, the good & the bad happened around the same period, & possibly right after each other.

Little acts of kindness, make the world a wonderful place. The time when you rear-end someone & the other person, inspected the damage, & said, "it's all right".

What makes you happy? Ice-cream yes, but I was looking for something a little more profound.

Right or wrong? Deep down, you know one from the other.

Death of someone you know, or even someone you did not know that well - makes emotions ebb & flow. You relate to it through similar experience you may have had with someone in your own family. You wonder if you will ever see this person again, & wonder about the soul & the after-life...

'Starry starry night' - your heart is so full as you gaze up. We attach so much significance to our own being, but in the larger scheme of the cosmos, we realize how insignificant we are, a speck in the cosmos.

You look around, & wonder why the world was created, where everything is headed, what is the purpose of Darwinian evolution, the purpose of volcanoes, humans & everything else happening around, & if there is grand purpose above all else. What a quagmire! With no answers yet.

When do you die? When you have resolved all the issues that are bothering you!

The dude, Buddha, seems to have found the answers to the questions of life. However, since he is currently dead, you cannot get your questions addressed. Maybe you could get your lawyer to subpoena him. If you do, let me know. I have a few things to ask him, myself.

Conclusion

Be healthy, make money, help fellow human beings, & make sure you have some fun along the way.

Hope you enjoyed reading the book as much as I enjoyed writing it. I plan to publish similar thoughts, every year. If you would like to leave a thought/ feedback or want a copy of the book, please write to stories@ncipb.com.